A NOTE TO PARENTS

Reading Aloud with Your Child
Research shows that reading books aloud is the single most valuable support parents can provide in helping children learn to read.
- Be a ham! The more enthusiasm you display, the more your child will enjoy the book.
- Run your finger underneath the words as you read to signal that the print carries the story.
- Leave time for examining the illustrations more closely; encourage your child to find things in the pictures.
- Invite your youngster to join in whenever there's a repeated phrase in the text.
- Link up events in the book with similar events in your child's life.
- If your child asks a question, stop and answer it. The book can be a means to learning more about your child's thoughts.

Listening to Your Child Read Aloud
The support of your attention and praise is absolutely crucial to your child's continuing efforts to learn to read.
- If your child is learning to read and asks for a word, give it immediately so that the meaning of the story is not interrupted. DO NOT ask your child to sound out the word.
- On the other hand, if your child initiates the act of sounding out, don't intervene.
- If your child is reading along and makes what is called a miscue, listen for the sense of the miscue. If the word "road" is substituted for the word "street," for instance, no meaning is lost. Don't stop the reading for a correction.
- If the miscue makes no sense (for example, "horse" for "house"), ask your child to reread the sentence because you're not sure you understand what's just been read.
- Above all else, enjoy your child's growing command of print and make sure you give lots of praise. *You are your child's first teacher — and the most important one. Praise from you is critical for further risk-taking and learning.*

— Priscilla Lynch
Ph.D., New York University
Educational Consultant

To Mary and Harriet
— C.S.

The editors gratefully acknowledge the
comments and advice of Dr. E. H. Colbert
of the Museum of Northern Arizona.

Text copyright © 1998 by Miriam Schlein.
Illustrations copyright © 1998 by Carol Schwartz.
All rights reserved. Published by Scholastic Inc.
HELLO READER! and CARTWHEEL BOOKS and associated logos
are trademarks and/or registered trademarks of Scholastic Inc.

Library of Congress Cataloging-in-Publication Data

Schlein, Miriam.
    What the dinosaurs saw/ by Miriam Schlein; illustrated by Carol Schwartz.
    p. cm. — (Hello science reader! Level 1)
    Summary: Describes what the world was like when dinosaurs roamed the
earth, and introduces many of the animals and plants in nature today that
were also seen by the dinosaurs.
    ISBN 0-590-37128-2
    1. Paleontology — Juvenile literature. [1. Paleontology.]
I. Schwartz, Carol, 1954- . II. Title. III. Series.
QE714.5.S35 1998
560 — dc21   97-12892
                                                                      CIP
                                                                       AC

10 9 8 7 6 5 4   8 9/9 0/0 01 02

Printed in the U.S.A.   24
First printing, January 1998

What the Dinosaurs Saw

ANIMALS LIVING THEN AND NOW

by Miriam Schlein
Illustrated by Carol Schwartz

Hello Science Reader! — Level 1

SCHOLASTIC INC.

Cartwheel
·B·O·O·K·S·®

New York   Toronto   London   Auckland   Sydney

Come with me.
We can see
things the dinosaurs saw
long ago.

We can see
a spider spinning,
same as the dinosaurs saw.

Two turtles resting
on a rock,
just as the dinosaurs saw.

We can see
three wiggly worms,
same as the dinosaurs saw.

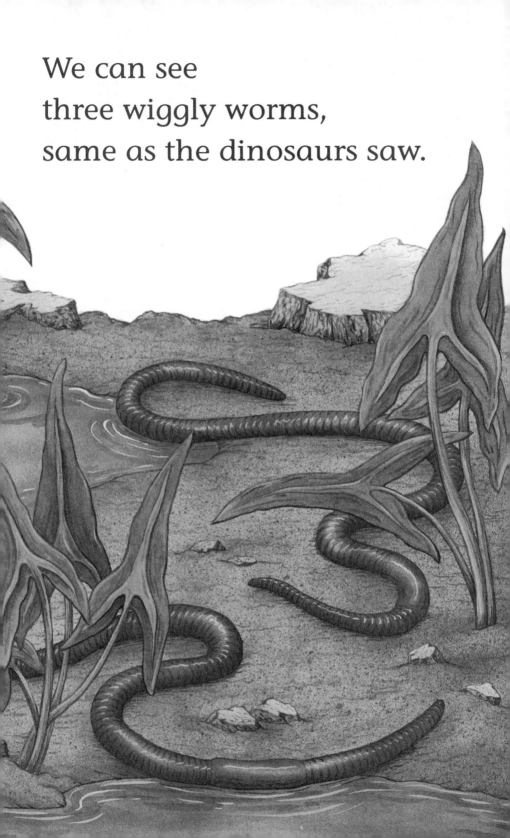

Four little pine cones
falling from a tree
was something else
the dinosaurs could see.

Five frogs croaking.
The dinosaurs heard that, too,
long ago.

Six snakes sliding...

seven salamanders sleeping...

eight gulls gliding...

nine possums prowling...

All these things
the dinosaurs saw

are still here
for you and me to see.

The sun that warmed
the dinosaurs
still warms you.

And the same moon
that shines down on you
shined down long ago
on the dinosaurs, too.